To Mark and Lia, who bring endless
wit, wisdom, love and inspiration to my life

Book design by Susan Verlander and Sara Gillingham.
Typeset in DIN Mittelschrift.
The illustrations in this book were rendered in Adobe Illustrator.
Manufactured in Singapore.

Library of Congress Cataloging-in-Publication Data
Verlander, Susan.
Wake up, City / by Susan Verlander.
p. cm.
Summary: Explores the sights and sounds of waking up in a city, from
alarm clocks ringing and birds singing to sidewalks filling and
jackhammers drilling.
ISBN 0-8118-4136-7
[1. City and town life—Fiction. 2. Morning—Fiction. 3. Stories in rhyme.] I. Title.
PZ8.3.V71264Wak 2004
[E]—dc21
2003007840

Distributed in Canada by Raincoast Books
9050 Shaughnessy Street, Vancouver, British Columbia V6P 6E5

10 9 8 7 6 5 4 3 2 1

Chronicle Books LLC
85 Second Street, San Francisco, California 94105

www.chroniclekids.com

wake up, city

SUSAN VERLANDER

chronicle books · san francisco

rring
aling
aling

alarms ring

birds sing

subways rumble

tummies grumble

toast pops

coffee shops hop

gourmet gourmet

shopkeepers sweep

commuters beep

buses start

messengers dart

traffic cops twirl

KLEEN SWEEP

street sweepers swirl

sidewalks fill

jackhammers drill

deliveries begin

meter maids grin

newspapers appear

morning is here!

beep
beep
beep

ring ring chirp r
pop gulp swis
zip tweet tweet s
chit chat c
slam oh no! o
woof hello! rin
grumble pop g
vroom zip twee